Hungry Monster

Story by Joy Cowley
Illustrations by Martin Bailey

Mom and Dad were asleep.
So were the children.

The monster banged on the door.
"Wake up. It's morning.
I want my breakfast," he called.

No one came.

Bang! Bang! Bang!
"Give me some food," he yelled.
"I'm hungry."

But no one came.

"Very well," said the monster,
"I'll go out and get myself
some breakfast."

Along the road he saw
a mailbox.

"Is that good to eat?" he said.
"Let me see."

Down went the mailbox.

Then he saw some roller skates.

Gulp, gulp!

"I liked them, too," he said.

Next he came to a bicycle.
"Now *that* looks good," he said.

Gulp, gulp!

He ate the bicycle, too.

Now the monster was full.
But on the way back,
he saw a red car.

He stopped and looked at it.
It was a big car.

"I'm not hungry," he said.
"But I do like red.
I'll have just a bite or two."

Gulp! He ate the door.

Gulp, gulp, gulp, gulp!
He ate the wheels.

"One more bite and that's all,"
said the monster.

He opened his mouth.

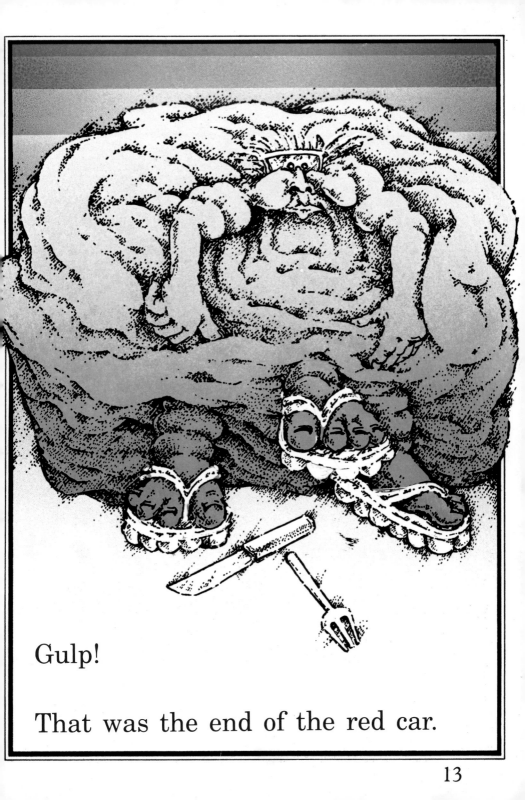

Gulp!

That was the end of the red car.

The monster went back home.
He got into his bed.

"Oh dear, oh dear," he said.
"I'm not very well."

Mom and Dad and the children
got up.

"Come on, Monster," they said.
"It's time for breakfast."

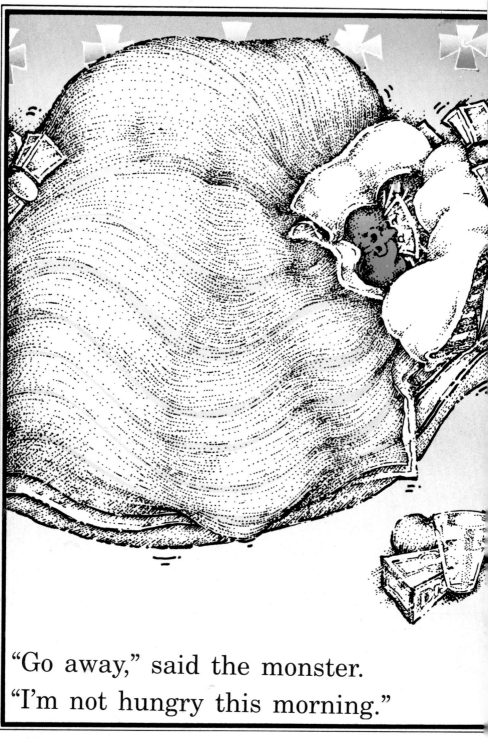

"Go away," said the monster.
"I'm not hungry this morning."